T0345525

The Law of Inheritance

THE ARAB LIST

The Law of Inheritance

Yasser Abdellatif

TRANSLATED BY ROBIN MOGER

LONDON NEW YORK CALCUTTA

Series Editor
HOSAM ABOUL-ELA

Seagull Books, 2018

First published in English translation by Seagull Books, 2018

ISBN 978 0 8574 2 545 4

British Library Cataloguing-in-Publication Data
A catalogue record for this book is available from the British Library.

Typeset by Seagull Books, Calcutta, India
Printed and bound by Maple Press, York, Pennsylvania, USA

Contents

Introductions

A MORNING LIKE THOUSANDS OF MORNINGS down the years far and near.

A boy: getting ready to smoke beside the school wall.

Not an addict. Smoking his sole means of registering protest at the mud-caked road that stretched from home to school and which, though he walked it every day, stayed changeless and tedious as clockwork.

He looked left and right to take in the lie of the land and, as he switched off for the first time to savour the initial hit, the hand of the pockmarked Arabic teacher landed heavily on his shoulder, catching him in the act:

Your father's off in Saudi Arabia . . .

You're the older brother . . .

Responsibility . . .

A good example . . .

Almighty Allah speaks the truth . . .

Sentences that go in one ear and out the other as he slips away from the present's panic and into that recent day when he'd gone to the airport in the company of younger brother and benevolent uncle to welcome back Father for a brief holiday.

The day his younger brother had escaped the benevolent uncle's grasp and got himself lost, a wraith between the legs of travellers and those waiting to receive them. A panic like the one he felt now had seized the uncle and off he had dashed, combing through the crowds until he'd found the boy with head wedged between the metal rails that fenced off the arrival hall. Papa! Papa! the little one had cried and in the distance: Father advancing, pushing a trolley laden with luggage.

The benevolent uncle, panting from his running hunt for the boy (the ward!), had embraced his brother while the young boy clung to his father's legs. And as for him: he'd shyly shaken his father's hand, noting the white hairs at his temples.

A year on, by the same wall, smoking hash this time and wearing a jacket whose style had given him doubts from the time it first arrived in that same luggage. He blows out blue smoke, each exhalation a pulse of rage directed at potential ambush: a threat to anyone who might catch him that this time he'd out their eye with the joint's coal. But the crater-faced Azharite instructor had drifted off to Saudi Arabia to instruct Gulf scions in their own tongue and teach them not to smoke in school.

THE MOTHER'S BROW is dewed with fever.

Husband absent, she raves, while at the bedside stands a badly behaved little boy, his younger brother balled uselessly beside him.

The mother's raving swells. He weeps in fright.

Dunya comes in, carrying cold-water compresses and her eighteen years like an angel of mercy.

She holds him to calm his terror and ministers to the mother.

The ten-year-old's nose between these breasts.

The very instant in which his mother is almost lost, Dunya slips between his skin. Beauty's compensation.

Dunya came carrying cold-water compresses to nurse his mother and took possession of his life for years thereafter.

THE ABSENT FATHER RETURNS from the Gulf with a car and dreams deferred and now, again, that long absence over, the family is in order.

Discipline. Where are you off to this evening?

The cinema with friends, a ready pretext for Thursday-evening wanderings.

With Mahmoud he goes to the dive in Old Cairo to smoke hash with labourers.

The first time they went he was nervous, scared of the place and the people; he smoked warily, afraid that, stoned, they might treat him roughly or make him the butt of their jokes.

He thinks of his mother making soup. Is this the cinema?

The warmth of home. What brought us to this den of thieves?

We're just two callow boys from one of the French schools.

But the workers babble on heedless and he and his friend sit tight, swapping through the intoxicated dancers a glance that is a glass raised to victory. They depart the dive, the rough men who've never known the heft of schoolbags weighted with homework.

Faculty of the Arts, Department of Philosophy. He writes short stories.

The girl introduces him to friends: members of Freedom Lodge.

Facing the leftists, he grips his shirt collar, straightens his clothes and clears his throat.

A ceaseless stream of cigarettes, Palestinian keffiyehs, Vees-for-Victory.

Dear comrade, the story's not bad at all but it's irredeemably subjective.

Perestroika . . .

Ceaușescu hasn't fallen yet . . .

Have you read *One Hundred Years of Solitude*?

The year before—his last year at school—the pretty art teacher had asked them to draw a picture 'on the theme of silent nature' and he had sketched Don Quixote's tomb, then leant a lance against it and on the gravestone wrote these lines by Naguib Surour:

> I am not numbered among the knights
>   of old
> when the knights of old are counted
> but mine was ever a knight's heart:
> hating the hypocrite and craven
> and loving what is true
> in equal measure.

And in the background, a whirlwind surmounted by a crow, signifying destruction. A crow, in the teacher's opinion, that was at odds with her chosen theme of silence.

Back home with his story as once he'd gone home with his picture. Trailing disappointment.

Hopes and dreams congested.

The art teacher, Freedom Lodge, Cairo University: Thank you all.

THE TABLE-TENNIS ROOM AT THE BACK of the schoolyard, next to the chemistry lab and abutting the rear wall of the school. From there, at break-time, door latched from the inside, they could leap down into life's broad embrace, buy cigarettes from a nearby kiosk and be back in time for class, and, occasionally, not be back at all. An oasis in a desert of discipline.

With his friend Hisham he'd knock the ball back and forth across the table. Hisham was useless but he was one of the rare souls who wouldn't make a racket and disturb the room's familiar calm.

The others are outside, busy with their football, and though playing in here isn't much fun, it's preferable.

Together they hear the familiar putter of an engine outside the school wall. Mohammed Suleiman, off school today, and the only one of them to own a motorcycle. They would ride escort to him like crippled tortoises on bikes with slipping chains.

They lean out over the wall. Why didn't you come today, Silmoun? Didn't fancy it, he replies and, hands on handlebars, breathes smoke from the cigarette which dangles from his mouth.

Give us a cigarette, Silmoun. Go on.

And calmly Silmoun counters that *he* has never taken a single cigarette off *them*, so why should he? Dropping back down off the wall, they hear the motorbike move away.

He looks at Hisham and asks him what Silmoun could have meant. Hisham says, *C'est la vie contemporaine*, *Monsieur*, incompetently batting the ball at him over the table and it lands askew and is lost in air . . .

On foot.

By night he crosses the suburb from its farthest point north, where home is, to the deep south: his friend's house. Mahmoud's bedroom window has been shut for nearly a year now.

He passes the window on the way to Nader, Mahmoud's neighbour and cousin, turning towards it with no little sorrow, a sorrow intensified by his conversation with Nader to cigarettes aglow in the balcony's gloom, to tea, and to music that retreats to the edge of consciousness.

Conversation dealing in reports: bulletins from the paths they've taken. Which faces have been seen. The torments of their friend Hisham in the wards of Qasr El Eini.

The last time he went to see him, Mahmoud was sitting at the desk in his bedroom, slumped forward, face-down and weeping, stating shamefaced that he didn't like being like this. He stood silently beside him. And when his mother had come in her red kimono, hands folded over her stomach, she'd looked at him over spectacles which had slid down to the end of her large nose and asked how he was doing, and he'd informed her that, at last, he had convinced Mahmoud to go to rehab.

YOU PLAY WELL, HE TOLD HIM, but you only care about building rallies. In table tennis what counts is points.

And once the school had decided to join the district sport leagues, he and his friends, the table-tennis-room group, were disqualified from representing the school: the administration, in the person of the games master, indicating it was well aware how this gang of delinquents were using the place. A gesture to the cigarette butts heaped in corners and a look to say that what had been left unsaid was worse still.

The school's more athletically gifted students formed teams for the major sports—basketball, handball, football (of course)—while table tennis was home to the semi-skilled, those who never frequented the main hall.

Since district rules stipulated that no student could compete in more than two sports, the volleyball team remained unsubscribed. The school harboured little hope of progressing in the competition because neighbouring schools numbered members of the national junior squad among their ranks. The volleyball team was just for the sake of completeness; to cast dust in their rivals' eyes. Someone on the administration said, Better to get those six first-year layabouts for volleyball than leave them out on street while the league's on.

They stood in their half of the court—a volleyball court they now saw!—and the opposing team's serves rained down unchallenged. Three of the players wore spectacles, let us not forget. Let us not forget Hisham, standing centre-court with his hands in his pockets, nor the fat kid too weak to lift his arms. That all six were smokers. The table-tennis-room regulars.

ONE

The Fascists

CAIRO CAN BE AN INSPIRING CITY, especially in winter. So I think to myself as I come home one evening. The microbus stops where the overpass descends to the street, rain pouring, Road 10 running beneath, the taste of a damp cigarette. Winter is, even so, like religion: both fit spaces for expressing emotion, sadness above all. A whistle lengthening then broken off: a soundtrack to the scene; a perfect summons to tender feeling for a tableau that has been generated thousands of times before and embedded in memory and which, when tickled by the tune, comes back to life .

Since waking this morning, I've felt as though I'm moving through a novel. From the moment my feet first touched the floor by my bed, feeling for the sandals through the murky aftermath of a four-hour sleep, then staggering to the bathroom and switching on the light despite the daylight seeping through the window.

Over the tap, a little cupboard for toothpaste and the like, its two doors mirrors opening inwards to face each other and grant you the most wonderful opportunity you'll ever get to see yourself twice mirrored.

Looking directly into a mirror, it's not yourself you see but how you feel about that self, in each and every instance granting the image before you a measure of beauty.

But look at yourself in one mirror via another and you see that self in isolation: you look to the right side of your face and see the left and vice versa; something outside yourself. But never allow yourself to spin out behind the endless reduplication of images, down the unbroken sequence of reflections—that might give the illusion of immortality.

Make do with the second reflection and you will learn to love that self of yours without blind adoration, to curb it when it grows beautiful, to subject it to your scourge and cleanse it of all that does not belong.

'You won't go mad and you're not going to try to kill yourself either.'

'Why not?'

'Because you've already tried it.'

Francoise Mackay, a French-Canadian. We met by chance and our chance encounters multiplied until we were obliged to meet on purpose: a single meeting lasting five hours. I had just emerged, exhausted, from a love affair and among the things I told her about myself, I told her this, and she, with her thirty-four years, with a woman's insight, understood what part she might play in my life. And didn't want to.

Speaking out of the first mirror, I'd say she didn't want to, but if I were to hold true to what the second said, then I must admit that it simply didn't appeal to her—to play that part with me.

Following that meeting—and despite its intimacy—she took to evading my attempts to meet again, until she vanished for good.

'I lived in France with the unhurried simplicity of the Quebecois. I was always trailing behind and then, just as I was beginning to adjust to a Parisian tempo, I'd had to return to Canada. It was too late to undo my newly acquired habits and so I always seemed to be in a rush, unable to stay put for any length of time. And now I'm here, nine months in Egypt, inshallah.'

Trying to picture the first girl you'll come across today and how the day will take shape accordingly: part of the morning's liturgy.

Underwear, pants, vest, shirt, pullover, another pullover, sweater. My hand emerging from my sleeve to grasp the metal bar fixed parallel with the carriage ceiling, and at the next stop the crowd inside the carriage doubling and me, teetering on one leg, the other kinked. On the saddle of my bent leg rides a girl. Crowd as cover. She wears jeans and a hijab on her head—bottom half liberated, top half temperate. Her thighs contract around my thigh and I can't help thinking that this is an injustice, that she can rub her female parts against my male thigh with impunity, but such thoughts don't stop the warmth spreading from my leg to the rest my body as she—confirming my view on her antonymous parts—goes on chattering hysterically to a companion, face turned away from the true connection: a body, gambolling in fresh pastures and decoupled from her vocal apparatus which remained with God, the passengers and her companion, hijab-clad like herself.

Out of the maw of the Metro's tunnel, the exit which opens onto Cairo's most celebrated pavement, the sidewalk past Café Ali Baba, Zed Cafeteria and the newspaper seller everybody knows.

Each time I travel up from Maadi to the city centre, I select a different exit from the tunnel, a different entrance to the city: Bostan Street, Tahrir Street, Qasr El Nil and Champollion and, most frequently, Talaat Harb. This time, I enter through Mohammed Mahmoud.

When Henry Miller returned to Brooklyn after his lost years in Europe, as he entered the street where his old house stood, he saw that the grocer's outside which he'd been beaten as a boy had become an undertaker's. For me, too, such chance discoveries have played their part in the transformation of places and their relationship to me. Say you turned into Mohammed Mahmoud: on your left, immediately after the American University, there's a domed building with a pointed archway over its gate. This building, kindergarten to the Lycée next door, is where I spent a portion of my childhood—while we were still living in my grandfather's house in Abdeen; before we returned to Maadi and I transferred to the school's branch there. During my early childhood, the kindergarten's domed edifice was painted pink, its small mosaic-tiled courtyard giving out onto the sandy playground of the main school through a little garden which was sectioned off by a dainty wooden gate. The arches over the classroom doors that ringed the tiled yard were also pointed. The quiddities of this roseate world lie over my childhood like a dream: the small fountain on whose surface bobbed lotus leaves, atop their broad expanse the frogs which we would warily harass with sticks; the little puppet theatre where Madame Georgette would put on shows in French, which of course we did not yet understand but enjoyed hugely all the same; the black piano on which Madame Nabila Habashi would play, nails always beautifully painted (how that younger me wished she would invite me home so I might see her in the clothes she wore there; and why I always imagined that she'd be wearing rings on her toes, I've no idea).

The shadows. How they'd overspread the pink walls, their lengthening associated somehow with the approach of home-time, when the man would stand ringing the bell in the little garden between the two yards and Mother would be waiting for me outside the entrance.

I pitched up here one early autumn morning in 1990. I'd taken a considerable quantity of sleeping pills and even so had been unable to sleep. I shall visit the cradle of my dream-like childhood, I told myself: maybe I'll find something to stir my memory. And I deceived the doorman, claiming I'd come to inquire about enrolling my younger brother at the kindergarten. He let me in. I found no trace of my memories there and so I departed, riding the train back to Maadi.

I mention Miller's story because the once pink kindergarten was grey now, not with age but thanks instead to a shrewd painter who chose the very colour that lets me stand here, twenty years on, and contemplate my early childhood.

What child now sits within this building who, in another twenty years, will stand here studying it? And what colour will it be then? Perhaps more fitting for the days ahead that it be black, its arched doors and windows painted red to match the American fast-food joints which face it from across the road.

Continue walking down Mohammed Mahmoud to the junction with Noubar Street and you will see it take on a different character, the first indication of this being its name, which changes here to Qoula Street; the second, that you are no longer in the neighbourhood of Bab Al Louq but in the heart of Abdeen.

Architecture alters and the street narrows slightly. Qoula is the birthplace of Mohammed Ali Pasha, grandfather to Khedive Ismail who built both square and palace.

Before Qoula Street meets Mohammed Farid Street (formerly Emad Al Din), and this time on your left, there is a narrow street—very cramped but called a street because it in turn plays parent to a tiny passageway whose name claims the prefix 'alley'. This alley-street and passage-alley share a name: Balaqsa.

This is home to the tomb of an anonymous Sufi saint dubbed Sheikh Hamza. When I was little it was here that my mother took me to buy wheat and rice from a store facing the tomb. It was the time of the saint's festival, a festival so limited in scope that all its paraphernalia—the swings, the fireworks, the tents—could be crammed into the tiny tract of street and alley.

At this festival I witnessed things I never since saw at any of the major festivals which I would seek out as a grown man (Sayyida Zeinab, say) where, given their vast size, details one might think of as essential are lost amid the crowds and profusion of incident.

This was the singular thing I saw, from a vantage-point level with my mother's knee: a crimson stall from whose opening leant a man with a great beard and, in one hand, a sharp implement like a razor which he wiped with a piece of cotton gripped in the fingers of the other.

I clung tighter to my mother and asked her what the man was doing. She answered, offhand: Circumcising. Thereafter everything was stained with red: the fireworks' flames, the tents, the trembling lights, and the blood—the blood now gushing in my mind's eye. What alarmed me most and whipped the whirl of questions in my young brain to a blur was that I'd seen them hand him not a boy but a girl, and thrust apart her thighs.

In this same street or alley, some fifty years before, lived Hanna, son of Saadallah the kerosene vendor. A legend. I never met him, of course, but I was told about him. I was told that Hanna had slept with most of the women in the alley, and while it's no great surprise that, from time to time, in such a place as this (or elsewhere), great lovers should be found, the Casanova of Balaqsa possessed none of the qualities for which the great swordsmen of his time were known: short and thin and pinch-faced in an era when beauty (before French standards took hold) was measured in terms of plumpness, his clothes forever smeared with kerosene from his father's workshop. On top of which he was a Christian.

Rodent-like, he lurked behind his greasy counter, welcoming in the alley women who made up his clientele. His tastes did not discriminate between the wife of a merchant and that of a sheikh or white-collar effendi, and he had a singular way of running them to ground. He lived in the alley, so he knew its residents, and would always begin by asking his chosen quarry how her husband was, and then, bit by bit, he would start to take on the mannerisms of that man, exaggerating them until he'd transformed him into a grotesque caricature in which the wife might perceive what lie her life was built on, demolishing in mere moments that institution whose mainstay was her helpmeet. Striking while the iron was hot, he would pay her a visit the very next morning—having checked the husband was absent—after which it was just a case of those simple, long-perfected strategies which placed the marriage bed, no longer sacred, within his reach.

This I heard from Miss Safiya: my grandfather's neighbour before his death, then ours after our move to 39 Mustafa Kamel Street in Abdeen, and, furthermore, a former lover of the dear, departed Hanna.

The story wasn't told to me but to my father, whom she treated as one of her own children: the child with whom she could sit up and gossip as she could not with her actual offspring.

She said, too, that for years her husband had puzzled over the significance of the kerosene with which she'd smear the pillow before they made love.

And I would listen, looking on as one who will later understand.

Miss Safiya had grown old, she was seventy or more, and with kohl-rimmed eyes would sit like

Sekhmet, goddess of war, enthroned in a big chair in her flat's hallway, front door open onto the stairwell, tracking the traffic upstairs and down with astonishment at the many strangers now passing through a building whose inhabitants, young and old, she'd once known so well. Chewing her lip, clapping the palm of one hand on the other's back in the gesture characteristic of traditional women, and muttering: 'All shapes and colours, like Samaan's book . . . '

I now know that Samaan was the Jewish millionaire who owned the chain of Sidnawi department stores, that the 'book' was a catalogue of fabrics and that three generations of Cairene history and language lay between me and Miss Safiya.

With the end of Qoula Street we reach Abdeen Square and stand directly facing the huge palace. The palace is a white edifice of low elevation and its gardens sprawl away for such a distance that the buildings beyond them cannot be seen. To someone standing in the centre of the square it forms a white horizon which meets squarely with the sky's blue.

In winter, as it is now, the space seems bathed in a perpetual moonlight. The muted strength of the sun, the palace's pale horizon line, that sprawling verdant lacuna: a vision that can be yours if you strip palace and place of their political and social significance; that is, if you strip them of their history.

I don't seek to escape my romanticism but I do try, as far as possible, to play it down.

Along the palace's southern wall runs Sheikh Rihan Street, leading eastwards to Port Said Street (formerly Al Khaleej Al Masri), which marks the divide between the neighbourhoods of Abdeen, Sayyida Zeinab and Al Darb Al Ahmar, and westwards to Tahrir Square. It was here, in a small passage branching off this street and parallel with the edge of the square, just a stone's throw from the palace, that my grandfather spent his early life before he and his family moved to 39 Mustafa Kamel Street, which also leads off Sheikh Rihan.

Their relocation from Geneina Lane to 39 Mustafa Kamel signified more than just a rung's rise up the social ladder; it was also evidence of a change in lifestyle. To be precise: a move from the ranks of the proletariat to that of the effendis. He'd started out as a barman at one of the clubs maintained by the political parties, and it was from this position—from behind the bar—that he had permitted himself to intervene in a conversation between a pasha and another grandee on the subject of Ahmed Amin's book, *The Dawn of Islam*.

The pasha was not especially interested in the conservative viewpoint voiced by the barman in objection to their own, nor was it so very unexpected to hear such views from the mouth of such a man. What got his attention was the existence of a Nubian cultivated enough to have read a recently released book such as Ahmed Amin's and, moreover, to have a full-formed opinion on the subject, however reactionary. It was at this point that the pasha learnt my grandfather possessed a certificate of primary education, which automatically qualified its bearer as an effendi, and so made up his mind to find him an administrative position at the party headquarters. Indeed, he promised to help him complete his education. And this may not have been the aristocratic condescension of a pasha to a poor-yet-cultured barman, so much as compassionate sympathy of a petty-bourgeois stamp, for the pasha was a former schoolteacher and had faced charges in the trial of the assassination of Lee Stack, sirdar of the Egyptian Army.

This transformation in the standing of my grandfather, which saw him move into the ranks of the white-collar effendis, was accompanied by another transformation, and one that affected him very deeply. Distancing himself from bar service allowed him to give free rein to his religious inclinations, to let them rise to the surface, and so, though maintaining his European mode of dress, he grew out his beard and shaved his lip.

His piety was not a part of the religiosity adopted by Egyptian liberalism in the thirties, which saw figures such as Taha Hussein and Al Aqqad become Islamist writers. It was instead his means of assimilating into broader society to which, with his features and skin colour, he remained a stranger; his way of integrating with what lay deeper than such differences. The liberal world on whose margins he existed—pouring drinks in its clubs, then working as an employee in the corridors of its political parties—did not at that time readily accept the idea of a Nubian effendi. The liberalism that produced men like Lotfi Sayyid was the same that brought forth the racist autocrat Ismail Sidqi.

But this sociological analysis, taking the so-called ghetto complex as its foundation, may be a touch unfair, so let us look for another, psychological or existential, which stands in relation to the first as the soul does to the law. More likely, the root cause of this religiosity was the mysterious psychological crises that would afflict my grandfather from time to time, and in whose wake he would confine himself to his room and speak to no one.

Despite the social stability and relative material comfort he enjoyed in his new job, he would fall prey to inexplicable bouts of depression, which would last for days at a time then fade away for his customary good cheer to gradually reassert itself. But on one occasion he went into a depression from which nothing could extricate him, though after a few days he was able (wordlessly) to go to work and (wordlessly) return, shutting his bedroom door behind him. As long as he was home he remained a prisoner there and never emerged.

And it was at this point that my grandmother had no other recourse but to send for Fathi, his nephew, for Fathi was the person closest to my grandfather and the keeper of his secrets. And duly summoned, Fathi arrived just days later and went into the room and the pair of them stayed put for hours, their seclusion undisturbed but for my grandmother, who from time to time would ferry them tea and biscuits.

At last a smiling Fathi emerged arm-in-arm with my grandfather, and took him on a tour of the cafes they used to frequent on their days off, meeting up with old friends and relatives. And by the time they returned late that night, my grandfather's sunny disposition was restored.

Though Fathi's uncle, my grandfather was at most just two years his elder for he himself was the youngest in a long line of siblings and Fathi was son of his eldest brother. On the eve of the First World War, having obtained their school certificates from the Al Dirr Primary School, they rode the same train to Cairo. They had left Nubia primarily in order to complete their studies but, swept up by currents of city life (which was itself undergoing violent upheavals at the time), they either chose—or were forced—to abandon formal education for the job market. They cycled through a number of the petty trades then available to Nubian immigrants in Cairo and their lives diverged on two parallel tracks. While my grandfather continued to educate himself, keeping pace with the evolution in his lifestyle (now a petty functionary in a major political party, with wife and children in a small flat in Abdeen), Fathi gave himself over entirely to a sensual existence and in the course of fifteen years managed to explore every byway of the city's underworlds, local and foreign alike.

Fathi's features resembled those of his uncle, the underlying structure of their faces the same, but while Fathi's grew bleaker, those of his uncle softened slightly, as though the difference was due to the way each lived his life.

By the mid-thirties, Fathi was working in one of the hotels in Suleiman Pasha Street and it was there that a fellow employee, a girl from the Italian community, fell in love with him. They conducted a passionate affair, provoking the ire of the girl's countrymen—Italian youths who'd fallen under the sway of Fascist ideology in their exile and who now resolved to murder the black man who'd so besmirched Roman honour. Seething with the right-wing rage that constituted the greater part of the political atmosphere at that time, and sheltered by the foreign privileges and mixed courts that the treaty of 1936 was yet to abolish, they took to riding black-shirted around Cairo on their motor-bikes, hunting for Fathi, until at last they came upon him sitting sipping arak in a bar at the

Boulaq end of Fouad Street (now 26th of July). The instant Fathi glimpsed the bikes through the bar's swing door, he leapt smartly out of the window, managing to get clear just as they were marching inside. They chased him the length of Fouad Street and into Al Sabtiya Al Jadida.

The legs that had scaled palm trees in his youth served him well when faced with the motorbikes of these young lions of the Axis. He vanished from their sight into the alleyways around the edge of Queen Nazeli Square abutting Ramses Station, and from there he fled to Alexandria, promptly boarding a boat to Rhodes where his physical strength and the few words of Greek he'd picked up from acquaintances in Cairo enabled him to work as a porter in the harbour. The harbour was a hive of activity, the workplace of dozens of travellers, most of them members of the intelligence services of various nations, who had descended on the island. When the island fell to the Third Reich, with the assistance of Fathi's old enemies, the Italians, a violent popular resistance flared up, backed by the British and Americans. Fathi stayed to see the last Axis soldiers leave, and no sooner had the war ended and maritime traffic returned to the Mediterranean than he set out for home.

This time he did not return to Cairo but journeyed south, to Wadi Halfa, capital of the Nubians and their greatest Nile port, where he opened a little store selling pots and pans. His decision to move so far away was not out of fear of Fascist brutality—the threat they posed was effectively ended following their defeat at the hands of the Allies—but rather to escape Cairo and the painful memories it held.

During a short rest-stop in Cairo, on his way south, people noticed a deep scar beneath Fathi's left eye . . . and thought better than to probe. The wound did no great harm to his dark good looks, indeed it lent them gravitas and dignity, and when my grandfather sat across from him, the scar seemed to balance out my grandfather's precociously greying beard, each man studying the addition to the other's features as though in contemplation of the years gone by. Learning of the store in Wadi Halfa which Fathi planned to open, my grandfather teased that he'd chosen a trade to keep him close to women. And Fathi did indeed travel to Wadi Halfa, and open his store, and marry a girl from his mother's side of the family, and father a boy and a girl, and there he stayed till 1961 when the waters of the High Dam rose to drown the entire town, and he was forced with others to move south once more, to Khashm Al Qorba in East Sudan. But that's another story.

The point is that my grandfather got religion.

I was never religious myself, with the exception of a single summer holiday just before we relocated from Abdeen to Maadi. I was ten years old and the move from one neighbourhood to another and from school to school meant the end of the little world I'd begun to weave around home and the classroom. I spent that holiday in the mosque. For those not bred to it, religiosity always surfaces in times of transition.

But I quickly constructed a new world in my new neighbourhood to whose basic components I added those ingredients peculiar to Maadi. Like the bicycle, for instance: an inner-city child's dream which can only be realized in the suburbs. The whole neighbourhood rode them and it was quite normal to see women setting off to the vegetable market on elegant bikes with front baskets, a sight that started to die out in the mid-eighties.

Then there was the move from one school to another. The old Lycée in Bab Al Louq was a cosmopolitan place, attracting the children of francophone communities, such as the Moroccans and black Africans, alongside Egyptian students from all over Cairo. A place where dialects, skin tones and cultures mixed. The Maadi branch was culturally orthodox, being almost exclusively limited to children from the suburb, most of them somewhere on the spectrum from upper-middle-class to not-much-lower. The transition from the mixed atmosphere of Bab Al Louq to the monocultural environs of Maadi felt somewhat comparable to the soul leaving its natural habitat to be exiled in history: a species of self-discovery through that self's suffering in an inimical environment. And then another exile, from Maadi to university: after finding yourself, you lose it again, gone missing in the subterranean halls of what, to the eyes of a shy teen from the suburbs, seemed like a bank of grey cloud.

Cairo University. A Babel of peacocks, depressives and the politicized, beards, intellectuals and pseuds, poets, seekers after the divine, sad-eyed girls in hijabs, half-prostitutes, full-blown prostitutes and a small number of beautiful girls—and all contained within an institution built on a hierarchy of contempt. The professors despised the students, the politicized students despised the other students (because they were leaders with an authority they maintained by force) and the intellectuals despised the ignorant. The students of the Arabic Department, most of whom belonged to Islamist organizations, despised the godless barbarism of the twentieth century, the modern-language students despised students from the other departments on grounds of class, while we in the Philosophy Department despised the lot of them, for we alone possessed universal knowledge. We'd walk the department's marble corridors declaiming the most resonant phrases in the history of humankind and writing them on the walls with black permanent marker: No man ever steps in the same river twice; Know thyself; Plato is dear to me; Good sense is, of all things among men, the most equally distributed; Man is a wolf to man; The world spirit ceased to be aware of itself as a self-aware entity; Minerva's owl spreads its wings only with the falling of the dusk. We repeated these terrible phrases unaware of their contradictions. We were playing at being sages, and you would not see us by day without cups of black coffee in our hands, the dark rings of sleepless nights beneath our eyes and youthful beards poking from our faces like thorns.

Early on in my university career, I attained a kind of Aristotelian faith in the presence of a prime mover behind creation. Somewhere at the back of my mind I held fast to God's attribute, 'The Helper': something to turn to in times of crisis. (During the Islamic philosophy class, the professor asked us the question posed by the great scholar of discourse, Ibn Al Ayadi, on the attributes of God—Are they real when applied to God and figurative when applied to man, or vice versa?—and we wracked our brains to find the answer and came up with nothing.)

Then it was the end-of-year exam and I hadn't slept for two nights and, at the desk in the hall, I suffered something like a collapse brought on by too much coffee and too many cigarettes and the information I'd stayed up all night memorizing evaporated from my head. I attempted to invoke my talisman, The Helper, but no help came. The hall, my fellow examinees, the Faculty of Arts, the whole of Cairo University—all of it vanished and I found myself sitting at a desk suspended in midair, the test now an existential one. I told myself to focus my mind and dredge up the answers I'd spent two nights revising and, gradually, my calm returned, my ability to concentrate came back, things were restored to their proper place all about me, from my pen the information flowed out onto the answer sheet and I passed both examinations.

The Sixties Generation:

His middle son was born after the sudden social elevation that made a white-collar worker of my grandfather and immediately preceding the outbreak of the Second World War; 1938, to be precise—just as Fathi was emigrating to Rhodes.

He graduated in 1961 from the Department of Production Mechanics at the Faculty of Engineering, Ain Shams University, and was assigned to military-sector factories: an engineer and a foot soldier for the heavy-industrial dreams of Utopian Nasserism, laying the foundation of a tomorrow whose sun was set to rise over an unbroken blackness. When these high waters had receded with the overwhelming defeat of 1967, and following the death of his brother Nasser, a schoolteacher, he left government service to try his luck as a free agent. From one failure to another and then, in the mid-seventies, he emigrated with many others to Saudi Arabia, to return a decade later, the man we saw arriving at the airport in the opening pages of this book, pushing the baggage trolley before him.

My ramblings have led me back to where I begun: Bab Al Louq.

The sun rose higher and noon drew near. Pain slowly awoke in my molar. It had first hit me a few days back and I had gone through a strip of painkillers before I decided to get it seen to properly. In Falaki Square, I went into a chemist's and bought a new strip, each pill walled with foil into its plastic cell. I pushed down on one. It answered to the pressure and quit its prison.

I reached Horreya Café. At the counter there I popped it into my mouth and filled a glass with water, staring hard into the eyes of the man standing there and putting on an air of casual indifference to allay his suspicions.

I sat in my favoured spot beside the window which looked out over a gloomy side street. I ordered a coffee despite knowing that coffee on top of painkillers is frowned on for risk it poses to the stomach lining. My need for caffeine was overwhelming. As things stood the day had not yet begun.

For a few moments I kept my eyes closed, trying to track the spreading effect of the painkiller as it travelled to the nerves of my rotten tooth. In the midst of my stupor, Saleh arrived with my coffee, set it down and withdrew. I came to again at the sound of two friends of mine, likewise unemployed, mocking me from the other side of the window:

'The philosopher's having a think. Let him be.'

'No, no! He's dressed like an *intellectual*, like Tawfiq Hakim.'

Come evening, I was laid out on the dentist's dreadful chair, trying to distract myself from the pain by staring down the cleavage that showed at her shirt's opening. She was working her drill around my doomed molar and a stench of powdered bone and burning rose to my nostrils. When she had finished, and while she was peeling off her plastic gloves, I said: Why do my teeth go bad one after the other when I take such care of them? It's inherited, she said firmly, It's in your genes, and dropped the gloves in a bin at her feet.

TWO

Pale Shadows of the Last War

THE STUDENT, THE SECURITY-SERVICE INFORMANT, stood with the transistor held to his ear, conspicuous amid the thousands who thronged the steps of the administration's building beneath the massive Doric pillars supporting the bronze dome where the Egyptian renaissance lay interred.

Cairo University, 1991.

The student demonstrations against the Gulf War went on for four days.

Beards the majority. Black bristles on chin and head dominating the scene. Rare patches of colour as various as the clothes they wore. The core of the crowd, Islamists, with their three subdivisions: the Muslim Brotherhood, the Islamic Group, then the most radical of all, Jihad, its device two crossed

Kalashnikovs over the Koranic verse cut short: *And prepare . . .*

The long head coverings of the Islamists' young women in mute tonal blocks, from black to white and grey between, occupied a sizeable area to the left of the scene.

The leftists and those from the nationalist right had outdone themselves, assembling these crowds for a student summit, which had been held in the university's square and from which the demonstrations had set out. Ageing leftist student and theatre obsessive, Ezz El Fayoumi, had mocked up a traditional mob shaming, moving between the faculty buildings beating a tambourine and surrounded by a troupe of his confederates all chanting the same bitingly satirical tirade. From faculty to faculty, numbers swelling as they made their way to the summit.

Whenever the pitch of fury rose and the roar seemed ready to blow the university's walls flat, the student informant would set in motion a rumour of hyperbolic implausibility, claiming it was news he'd just picked up as he surfed the foreign stations: Libya has joined the war alongside Iraq . . . Iran, too . . . Saddam has started bombarding Tel Aviv with Scud missiles . . . In an instant the angry chants would turn to joy unbounded and the storm clouds scatter.

As the march began, I was overwhelmed by loneliness, as though aware of my alienation for the first time. And between the crowds appeared Buthaina, the wicked witch, and started chattering to me in a state of high excitement. But I was unable to hear what she said because the chanting voices were growing louder and also for what we might call internal reasons, reasons peculiar to me. I followed the movement of her hands as they rose and fell in an excess of agitation, then, narrowing my gaze, I saw it, lurking beneath her enthusiasm: the frigidity of a girl from between whose thighs they'd ripped out life's transistor. I fought off a powerful desire to hug her, and why the desire came over me at all I don't know, nor why I repressed it.

Seif Al Din Mouza, a member of the Pioneers student group, was sitting between two girls on a path by the faculty of literature. The girls were of a type, their blue jeans and white shirts an attempt to approximate the Pioneers' uniform, and as the demonstration passed them by, and as Seif Al Din leapt to his feet, both girls grabbed him to prevent him hurling himself to his destruction. I must go with them! he cried out in distress and repeated the attempt twice more, the girls clinging on all the while. At last, and following a third effort, he collapsed weeping onto the shoulder of one (the prettier) who cradled his head and started caressing it with a maternal tenderness. In moments like these, such behaviour's to be forgiven.

Approaching two in the afternoon, the security forces surrounding the university started firing tear-gas canisters to break up the demonstration. These were metal tubes, very similar to cans of domestic insecticide, except heavier, and were shot from specially modified rifles to arc up thirty metres over buildings and walls and drop into the university's gardens and courts where they would discharge their gas to blind eyes and set throats and faces aflame.

It wasn't the tear gas that bothered me so much as a dread that from this deluge of metal tubes one might land on my head. I knew that a similarly innocent-looking canister had struck a student during the Suleiman Khater demonstrations at Ain Shams University in 1986 and killed her on the spot. So I ran, gaze flicking between sky (to avoid the bombs) and earth (to see my way), and as I ran, I glimpsed Ashraf Gazzar, a friend of mine who had contracted polio as a child, lying on his back in Lovers' Garden, halfway between the faculties of literatures and the political sciences. With trembling hands, Gazzar was groping over the grass for his metal crutches while two canisters squirted smoke beside him. I wished with all my heart that I could have rushed over and saved him, but my fear of the canisters—now raining down with particular intensity over the area around University Square—made me go on running. Self before selflessness, as a general rule.

My headlong flight had brought me to the central court of the faculty of commerce and by the cafeteria's wooden huts I sat on the pavement, a broken man. A few seconds later, a friend whom (for reasons of my own) I had dubbed Yohannah the Walker appeared before me. Yohannah, bright red from the gas, was hunting fruitlessly around the cafeteria for water to wash his burning face. The workers had closed their counters and fled and all the poor guy could find was a tower of stacked yellow boxes full of Schweppes. He yanked out two of the bottles and, smashing them open on the kerb, began to rinse his face in the bubbling liquid. I was watching this in astonishment, mouth agape, when I was startled by a loud cackling. It was our mutual friend Tareq Al Assyouti, seemingly materialized out of thin air. And Tareq went on laughing, so that when he eventually and smilingly cursed Yohannah and Yohannah's mother and opined that tear gas was a hundred times kinder on the face than washing it in orange soda, his words came out as a croak.

Tareq had barely finished when a fresh canister landed at his feet. Once again I was gripped by a terror that no laughter could keep at bay and we began to cast about for somewhere that might shield us from the law's long hand. An idiotic line of reasoning led us to the following: that the best place to hide was closest to where the canisters were being launched. The frontline! A regular stone wall of shoulder height topped by a palisade of green-painted iron spikes ran round the entire perimeter. We decided to dig in behind the university's north wall, directly facing the column of Central Security troops.

Once crouched behind it, a war of words broke out between Tareq and Yohannah over the Gulf War, with Tareq likening the conflict to the war between Sparta and Athens. Yohannah asked him which of the two was meant to be Kuwait and which Iraq—on what, exactly, was he basing his comparison?—and Tareq said that Iraq was Sparta, because its soldiers were valiant warriors, while Kuwait was of course Athens, because it had become the refuge of contemporary Arab philosophers and sages, from Abdel Rahman Bedawi and Zaki Mahmoud to Fouad Zakariya and Abdel Fattah Imam . . . and off he went listing names.

What is this idiotic conversation to me? I asked myself and fixed my eyes on the sky, following the gas trails overhead.

A few moments went by.

Then I was stunned to see Tareq jumping onto the stone half of the wall. It struck me that on a day like today, he wouldn't have neglected to bring along a full bottle of Parkinol tablets. Tareq stood on the stone wall, hanging from the iron railings and, from where we sat beneath him, Yohannah and I asked him to describe what was going on the other side. Tareq started to tell us what he saw. His voice, I noted, was a little louder than it should have been. He was more or less shouting. He said he saw a high-ranking officer, face hidden behind dark glasses and carrying a walkie-talkie linked directly to operational command—that he should know this came as a surprise—and he saw a long line of Central Security troops standing on the central divider in Bayn Al Sarayat Street. They were dressed in black, like chess pieces . . . Then he started screaming. They were melting onto the pavement like candles! Tareq paused for a moment, looked down at us with a face drained of colour and said that the officer had removed his automatic from its holster, discharged a bullet into his own head and had then toppled over, drenched in blood, between the black wax stubs of the soldiers. It was at this moment that Yohannah and I realized that the Parkinol was in full effect and that Tareq was raving. At exactly the same time, a rubber bullet (a real one, this time) struck Tareq in the thigh, and we had to take him to the student hospital for treatment.

Tareq Al Assyouti wasn't his real name, but I thought to give it to him here because it has the same ring to it as the moniker of an old terrorist who once sold his high-ranking friend for four pieces of silver. Of course, Tareq never sold any of his friends, but he said something not dissimilar in a short Haiku of his that ran

I don't know why God
did not deign to fashion friends
in the shape of coins

These few lines were greatly celebrated within the university's literary circles. An important poet, it seemed, had turned conventional morals on their head.

The point is that the day after the demonstrations, Tareq Al Assyouti had become a hero, borne aloft on shoulders with his jeans ripped upwards off the knee to display a portion of his gauze-wrapped, wounded thigh. He wasn't chanting himself, just silently gripping an empty gas canister, waving it back and forth, surrounded by chants in which Islam blended with Iraq and the poor, calls to bring in the Egyptian Army and curses on the state, the security services, America and Israel.

Yohannah the Walker had thrown himself wholeheartedly into proceedings and I didn't see him again as I wandered aimlessly around the university. He materialized again at midday on Day Three to ask if we could swap jackets because the security services had made a note of the colour of the one he wore, and so we did.

The day the protests came to an end, I asked Yohannah to give mine back and he returned it covered in gore. He himself didn't have a scratch on him, and to this day I've no idea whose blood it was that stained my jacket.

On the first day of the riots, a student from the Department of Law by the name of Khaled Abdel Aziz Al Waqad had been killed when a battle broke out at night between students living in the university residences and members of the security services posted at the university's north wall, which ran parallel to Bayn Al Sayarat Street and faced the residences. The young man had gone downstairs in his pyjamas to get a cup of tea from the little stall by the main gate and was struck by the fatal bullet—a live round this time, since night fighting is always more vicious, taking place, as it does, while history sleeps.

Four years after these events, I was at the gate of the A Step Along the Way military base, waiting to pick up the certificate that would exempt me from military service. I met a thin young man with a sparse beard and a prayer bruise in the process of taking shape on his forehead, suggestive of a recently acquired dedication to regular prayer. He was attempting to slip in through the camp gate with another youth who looked as though he could have been his younger brother. When the guard at the gate stopped them and said entry was only for those who'd been called up, the bearded man informed him that he was a soldier, same as him. The guard gestured at the beard with outright derision. How could you be? he said and turned away to continue with the security checks.

We stood together at the gate and the bearded boy started telling me about his military service which he'd spent fighting alongside the international coalition in Desert Storm: how he'd been seconded as a driver to the Saudi armed forces and then been wounded in the leg by shrapnel, after which he'd come back to Cairo to lie in a military hospital with no hope of treatment. And when his service was up he'd left the hospital as he was, his condition in no way improved. Semi-paralysed, in fact.

Receiving advice to demand treatment at the expense of the Saudi government on whose section of the front he'd been injured, he sent off a telegram to King Fahd in which he laid out his story, and the monarch invited him to be cured at the kingdom's cost in the hospitals of Riyadh. Because the invitation had been sent to his Egyptian army postal box, the Egyptian army sent him to Riyadh under cover of a military assignment, where the Saudi army met him and packed him off to one of the capital's luxurious infirmaries. And here he was, walking on his own two feet once more despite the platinum pin inside his leg.

He said he'd been cured undercover just as he'd fought *under cover* in the trenches at . . . ha ha ha . . .

The sands around the camp blotting up his chuckles the way the desert blots up blood and tears.

THREE

Maadi, Summer of '88

EACH 10 ML CONTAINS:

Chlorpheniramine maleate	3 mg
Phenylephrine hydrochloride	5 mg
Ephedrine hydrochloride	5 mg
Dextromethorphan hydrobromide	15 mg

Dr Mowaffaq, proprietor of the Mercy Pharmacy raised his eyebrows aloft as he read the insert for the Tosifan-N—which we referred to as N, for short—and folded it back inside the box. Six bottles, he said. You must be having guests round tonight. There were six of us in fact; I was the one who had volunteered to deal with him today. Outside, lurked five skeletons—propped against parked cars, sat on the pavement, chasing their tails not knowing what to do with themselves, all awaiting the result of this uncertain engagement with a new chemist: his willingness to swallow the bait, to connive or to turn the deal down wholesale and leave us to resume our wretched quest elsewhere.

When I emerged carrying the plastic bag with its load of six bottles, the skeletons jerked upright, bodies and souls reabsorbed, returned to them.

The bottle's golden glass a window onto the red liquid. Palms, dampened by strained nerves, gripping the tin cap at the bottle's mouth and—sweat on smooth metal—fumbling repeatedly before getting a grip and corkscrewing it off.

The dose drained in one gulp (empties tossed to the side of the street) and, at the end of Road 15, directly after the convent of Notre Dame des Apôtres and across the way from the wall of the St Leon Seminary, in whose spacious garden the monks had relinquished their right to play football to make way for a home for elderly priests, at the exact point where Maadi's southern boundary meets Tora: Mahmoud's house.

Mahmoud's family had rebuilt the property wall, the scrubby trees replaced by a barrier of white stone. The construction work had left a small pile of sand heaped outside. By setting a severed tree trunk on its side beside this pile, we fashioned the perfect spot for six young men, from nineteen to twenty-two years old, to sit.

It would take no great effort to recognize in them the old volleyball team, with a couple of players substituted out: one who'd passed his exams with flying colours and gone on to study medicine, the rigours of academia distancing him from his former schoolmates—'the wrecks' as he called them, whether in jest or earnest; the other enrolled at the Police College where he'd spend three-quarters of the year to emerge each vacation a person altered in proportion to his steadily mounting sense of power.

It took between twenty and forty minutes for the N to start working. Four would stay put by the sand pile and two volunteers would make the trek over to the desert wastes around Koutsika to buy block from Umm Amal with the fifteen pounds scraped together from the pennies in our pockets: the price of an *qirsh* of hash.

To reach Koutsika we had to cross the train yard adjacent to Tora Al Balad Station, where the Metro line to Helwan met the mine-ore tracks snaking out from Abbasiya and over the desert around the Autostrad which ran past at the back of the seminary. The train yard was a vast plot of land crosshatched by a maze of rails where dozens of old trains sank into decrepitude. It was home to foxes and stray dogs, to the dilapidated carriages adopted as dwellings by the first generation of street children, their numbers growing day by day as we trudged back-and-forth. We would often see them sharing out the haul they'd stolen or begged, and once we watched as they sat around a great feast of kebab meat, never neglecting, amid the rampant gobbling and slurping, to set a meat-stuffed loaf aside for the watchman. Those of us who saw the cup half full said, It's solidarity with their fellow proletarian; those who saw it half empty, It's protection money, brother.

Umm Amal sold two kinds of hash—the first a low-grade dust for *gouza* pipes which she wrapped in red cellophane, and the second an oily block for rolling joints wrapped in yellow—the second two pounds dearer per *qirsh* than the first. The first was called Pure with Thanks; the second, Your Satisfaction, O Lord. We'd buy a *qirsh* or half a *qirsh* of Your Satisfaction, with its pleasant taste and aroma, and by the time we'd returned the N would just be starting to take effect, that moment when the gooseflesh reached the user's head and surmounted it like a wreath, delicious prickling working the brain from within.

Nader began to break the hash into the crumbled cigarette tobacco using a bowl Mahmoud had fetched from his balcony, as though kept there for the purpose. The trip was just beginning.

It had been on just such an evening that, from our spot by the sand, we'd spied Esam Nagi approaching, mounted on his younger brother's twenty-four-inch bicycle: an absurd sight, with his bulk sagging down around the child-sized frame. To us, he was a half-welcome guest, half-tolerated on account of the affection we bore him (and him, us, beyond a doubt)—but because he had drifted apart from us as our interests diverged, he was also numbered among the strangers, our affection preserved in the memory of a once-living friendship whose echoes were confined between the walls of a school situated in a time and place not so distant from the time and place in which we sat.

As Esam pulled up, the spectre of nostalgic fondness with which we'd clothed him dissipated. He tossed the little bike into the sand, drew himself upright, dripping with sweat, and, without waiting to catch his breath or greet us, lit a cigarette: How you doing, boys?

Nader handed him a joint—Here you go—and Esam chucked away his cigarette, lit the joint and proceeded to smoke it *en seul*, violating the unwritten rule that joints be passed around equally and in strict order. He got straight to his point. With the air of someone springing a happy surprise he announced: What do you say to a free day at the seaside?

An extremely peculiar idea at first, but more agreeable once he started to explain. In the morning, Esam said, he was making a trip on behalf of the company where he worked to Ain Sokhna on the Red Sea coast and he'd be all on his own in the microbus with the driver. The six of us could go with him and spend the day at the beach. Faced with such a tempting offer there could be no prevarication. Each of us had to bring his beach clothes from home, Esam said, and, if possible, a bite to eat.

Finishing the joint he'd taken from Nader he said he'd drop by at 6 a.m. with the microbus. Same place. Then he picked up the bicycle, mounted and was once more a flabby and comical figure moving away beneath the glow of the streetlamps into the depths of Road 15.

A single dilemma consumed us: How to secure a supply for the trip? We didn't have much cash and the sympathetic pharmacies would be shut for sure. The owner and employees of the only night-shift pharmacy possessed a moral integrity sufficient for every pill-dispenser in the neighbourhood and, being chemists of long experience, they knew every trick young men like ourselves might try to throw them off the scent.

Sharif said that he had just come down from Luxor where he was studying hotel management and, among the many new discoveries he'd made, was a drug originally designed to treat Parkinson's. Parkinol. He claimed that it caused incredibly vivid hallucinations, similar to what we'd heard about LSD, which meant we'd have to treat it with caution and respect. In addition to which, it was cheap, unbelievably so: just a pound for a full bottle which held enough pills to send us all to dreamland for days.

An excellent idea, particularly since the drug wasn't yet common knowledge among users and had not been added to the list of tranquillizers and medicines that could only be purchased with a prescription. It would make the process of fooling the pious owner of the night-shift pharmacy all the easier. So we made up our minds and set about dividing up the tasks as we always did: one team going and another staying behind.

In the far distance, the purchasing delegation could be seen returning and, when their silhouettes had drawn closer, we saw one of them—Sharif—toss something into the air and catch it in his hand. And when they were closer still we could see that this thing was the magic bottle, and we congratulated ourselves on the success of our venture and knew that Sharif must have put on a convincing show to trick the veteran behind the counter. This accomplished, the trip would be a breeze.

About two hours before Esam was due, we were assembled at the spot, all set and ready to go. There'd been a protracted debate over just when we should begin our trial of the Parkinol, a debate that had been won by the impatient. Mahmoud had thrown down a full bottle of chilled water from his balcony and each of us had necked his pills, doled out by our resident expert Sharif.

The Parkinol pills were white and very small, which lent them a deceptive innocence. We had swallowed Sharif's dose and an hour or more had gone by without anyone feeling the slightest effect and so, doubting the veracity of Sharif's information, we'd each had more.

Another hour, and now the microbus was travelling through the desert along the Red Sea Road, Maadi and Qattamiya behind us. Esam Nagi sat up front with the driver, eyes puffy from a short nap and drinking tea from a plastic cap that doubled as a lid to the thermos which lay on the dashboard before him. The driver was smoking.

The six of us were distributed between the bus's twelve seats, a couple stretched out along their share of two seats each and four sitting side by side in pairs.

I was resting my head against the glass, enjoying the tickling buzz as the vehicle's juddering ran from window to skull and gazing through the window as the small dunes by the road rose and fell, rose and fell . . .

Heading due east at that early hour, the light shone directly through the windshield, forcing my eyelids lower, and for just a few seconds, or so it seemed to me, I slept. When I came to again, I knew from the strength of the sun that it was still rising and the journey, hardly yet begun, seemed to me to be a journey without end. I blamed the sweltering heat on the coastal sands, on the eye-reddening salt of the Red Sea air and on the exhaustion we felt after two days without sleep. What do we want with beaches and swimming? I asked myself. Aren't we just six junkies who sleep all day and spend our nights between Mahmoud's sand pile and the Mercy Pharmacy, precocious prisoners of despair? Despair. the word rang in my head: despair . . . despair . . . despair . . . its *s* an endless, echoing hiss, no sooner fading than whistling out anew, and then it began to take over my entire head, its letters plain before me, first separate, then joined, the echo dinning on until it seemed to me I had taken in a whole bookful of woe.

My throat felt dry as a twig. I told myself I'd fetch a glass of cold water from the fridge. Only then was it clear once more that we were in a tin box cutting through the eastern desert to the sea.

Daylight lent the vehicle's interior a soothing air. All of sudden I was playing chess with a friend, our small magnetic board on one of the bus's narrow seat-tops. The game was completely incomprehensible to me and I'd no idea when I had begun it or which of us was playing with which colour, nor could I tell with any degree of accuracy who my opponent was: Mahmoud? Mokhtar? I picked up a piece and squeezed it in my palm. It felt repulsive, loathsome, and even now I don't know how something as unremarkable as a chess piece could have been so vile to the touch. Frightened, I dropped it onto the small board's magnetic metal surface and as it landed it made a terrifying clang and rocked, booming, back and forth between the other, upright pieces. I lifted my head to my friend and he calmly turned away to the window beside him. For no reason that I could fathom, he burst into tears. Outside, the dunes still rose and fell. I looked to the front and watched Esam Nagi, face in profile with a pair of dark glasses over his eyes, smoking from the cigarette that never left his hand rising from his mouth and nostrils as he and the driver chattered on, deep in a conversation I couldn't hear.

We reached the seaside and the six of us got down as though stepping from a spacecraft onto the surface of the moon. In a state of complete disequilibrium. Beneath our feet the ground felt fluffy as wool.

When the great furrow that is the Red Sea first split open, a chain of flaming mountains sprung up on either side, red rocks beneath the roasting sun. The asphalt road we'd come by, running parallel to the coastline as far as Al Quseir and beyond, divides the shore from these peaks. I had my eye on a gaping black mouth in the mountainside when out of it leant . . . something. A dog, I thought at first: dun-coloured, its huge body blotched with black. But when I saw the size of its muzzle and the crook in its back legs, I knew it. The hyena slipped gracefully down to the foot of the slope, over the road and advanced towards a dead donkey that lay swollen on its back with its four legs frozen skywards.

Where'd I seen that carcass before?

It jammed its snout into the distended belly, worked its razor-toothed jaws and, straining every muscle in its mouth and neck, ripped out a large strip of flesh. Syrupy blood slid down from the corners of its mouth and soaked its grey-brown neck while its eyes rolled back in demented ecstasy. I was so captivated by the scene that I had failed to spot a pack of its relatives descending from the same cave. Slowly, surely, they began to advance. I watched them ignore the donkey banquet and come on, trotting towards us, bodies canted sideways as though their hind legs were racing to overtake their front paws. Creeping closer to our cooking fire, I carefully picked up a flaming branch in readiness. The others huddled together, back to back. Only the driver remained as he was, the cigarette never leaving his lips. Don't worry, he said, they don't attack the living. Who told you we're the living? someone replied.

The hyenas had formed a circle round us and begun to growl through their fangs. I heard someone speak and thought the driver had given another warning. I turned and asked if he'd said anything, and he answered with a derisive smile that he hadn't opened his mouth. I turned back. Not a trace of the animals. I faced him again: Where's the dead donkey? Still smiling he said, In your head.

I recall, too, the frozen hamburger patties thawing, ice melt soaking the sand and the taste of the bread I tried to chew my way through, struggling to swallow it as though it were cotton wool. And how we spent our day by the sea, I couldn't say. I recall lying in the shade of the bus seeing the sun drop over the horizon in one swift movement; being unable to stop myself staring at that red disc which, the next instant, had burnt a green circle on my eye, and then, after that, the whistling sound in my ears that lasted the rest the trip.

Nader, Mahmoud, Sharif, Mokhtar and Hani were lost in their own private dances. The driver was looking on like someone watching a farce. Something he couldn't understand. Only Esam Nagi enjoyed the trip, swimming and diving and eating.

Around midday, the otherwise deserted beach was visited by a second bus carrying a group of young Asians, most probably from the Philippines. Without ado, they took off their clothes and climbed into bathing costumes and, speechless, we looked on as young women went dipping like fish through the calm sea. I recall the driver breaking the silence, hitherto disturbed only by the distant sounds of the young visitors splashing around: Those Filipinos know how to enjoy themselves. They know how to get the best out of things even though they do the worst jobs. Domestic servants, things like that.

The recurring themes of that day's hallucinations:

Convinced a cigarette was wedged between your fingers and suddenly realizing your fingers were empty. Looking around and getting to your feet. Patting down your clothes and gaping at the spot where you'd been sitting. Your bewildered gaze meeting the grins of others who'd fallen into the same trap before you.

Lizards and insects. From time to time someone would cry out in alarm, flapping at the snakes and bugs he could feel crawling over his body. This entomological aspect led Parkinol's dedicated consumers (once its use had spread through drug-taking circles in the early nineties) to refer to it as Cockroach—Let's cockroach, they'd say—in the same way that Comital was known as Skulls or the potent tranquilizer Ativan was called The Southern Train in reference to that notorious incident in which a Southerner managed to drug an entire carriage by dosing drinking water with Ativan, then selflessly passing it around and robbing them of their possessions as they flew off to feast with blue angels.

Then the great snake twisted round to spit its poison (a poison that was itself the antidote) into the cup of the world, the cup of the world afloat on an ocean of pharmaceuticals. The late eighties was the golden age of chemicals. The hashish empires were coming apart in what was known as the great hash crisis, with weed brought into circulation as a local alternative. The millions of dollars which had formerly been frittered away overseas in pursuit of block now returned to the home market, and so it was that green stalks and bud made their contribution—in one form or another—to the process of economic reform that began with the onset of the nineties and ended with its end.

And as easily as one closes an eye and opens it, our day by the Red Sea was over. As the shadows came down, we set about preparing for the journey home. A feeling that we had done wrong possessed us all, prompted perhaps by the subconscious whisperings that had permeated the fog of day and made that empty shore their stage. And maybe it was the presence of Esam Nagi and the driver that broke the skein of fantasy over which we skated. We had gazed on blood and slaughter, orgies and forbidden things, all that lay neglected in our lives now laid out before us. And on the way home, the microbus moving down the darkened road, silence reigned. Most of us had sobered up, or almost, and when, from his corner at the back of the bus, Sharif called out for help, we rushed to him. He was hallucinating a nosebleed but we managed to reassure him that he was still high—and no wonder, for nearly all of us had taken far too much.

We had returned, and I had returned from that journey to this one, here: back at the sand pile, having smoked nearly half the *qirsh* we'd bought. Rock music was blaring from Sharif's tape deck which we'd propped up on the white wall of Mahmoud's house looming behind us. We were listening to Ronnie James Dio, the American heavy-metal singer who migrated from band to band over his career. He was singing about the night, about a darker night, about those who stood at the end of the line, about the curse that struck the world, about the nations who prayed that their days might end, about worlds in which your life dribbled away before your eyes. And the drumming, despite a violence that held real rage, maintained a metronomic beat, because the man belonged to the old school, to a venerable tradition he upheld until the end of the eighties.

There was a break after the song or maybe the tape had run out and nobody could be bothered to turn it over. Or perhaps they didn't want to risk breaking the spell by beginning a new track. Silence, violent after the music's violence, and it was minutes before we could make out the creak of crickets and frogs croaking. The street was sunk in darkness, wan lamplight leaving it murkier still, and it stretched noiselessly away before us, fenced in by the grandeur of the convent and cemetery whose high walls framed each side with the ranks of cypress and camphor trees that ran their length. And from the depths of that silence, from the far end of the convent wall, a sharp sound reached our ears. Like a woman's scream. We scrambled to our feet. There, where the wall turned the corner, sat a Peugeot 305, and beside it a young man struggling with a conscript who we recognized as one of the convent guards. Inside the vehicle a woman sat sobbing, her seat-back pushed down into the semblance of a bed. All this we saw by the glow of the car's cabin light, lit up by the opening of the door where the youth stood wrestling with the conscript.

We had no doubt that it was the woman who had screamed. It seemed clear to us what was happening, but all the same we intervened and asked the conscript, our neighbour, what was going on. He'd caught the young master riding the miss, he told us, and he'd got hold of *this*, and he waved a piece of triangular cloth in the air: underwear, no less. He swore up and down that he'd hand them over to the first patrol that drove by. The owner of the car was doing his best to act as though he possessed an authority that trumped that of the conscript's superiors, though his fear and his efforts to master it were plain to see. We took out cigarettes and gave one to the soldier and one to the young man, then reminded the conscript that God enjoins discretion and forgiveness whenever possible. We assured him that neither the young man nor the woman would do anything like this again. Anger ebbing, the conscript loosened his grip. Just for our sake, he'd let them go. The youth leapt into his car, switched on the engine and stamped the accelerator down as his left foot left the brake. The rear tires spun with a speed that outstripped their capacity to grip and they whisked free of the ground, whipping up a great cloud of dust and then, as the car levelled and settled, they held and it shot forward in what the kids call 'an American start'. He didn't switch on his headlights.

We stood there, coughing and brushing the dust from our clothes and heads, muttering about good being repaid with evil and cursing the religion of the young man and his mother (whom we'd never met). And when the dust had subsided, we saw that the conscript was still holding the young woman's panties. We succumbed to bout of hysterical laughter and, humiliated, he tossed the underwear into the bushes with an angry jerk. The six of us withdrew to our spot and when one turned back to look, he saw the soldier returning to retrieve the panties from the ground and cautiously tucking them into his uniform.

FOUR

Ahmed Shaker
or
The Foster-Son

SHAKER WAS RELATED TO MY GRANDFATHER, a fourth or fifth cousin, degrees of separation that are rendered irrelevant in the distant villages of the south by tribal factionalism and ties of loin and womb.

Slender of face, its blackness at odds with the usual light brown of the Nubian, Shaker came to Cairo in the thirties after his people had been displaced and pushed on into fresh exile: a place with no place for him. So Cairo it was, where my grandfather and his nephew Fathi had settled nearly twenty years before and where they now had homes and families.

Shaker had no education save that offered by the Koranic schools, known as 'cells' in the villages of Nubia, their sheikhs no better than the pupils at pronouncing Arabic with their Nubian accent which lightens emphatic letters and muddles genders. But Shaker spoke Arabic well and quickly mastered the dialect in Cairo where my grandfather, with help from his connections, found him a job as a tea-boy in one of the small banks owned by resident foreigners.

Shaker rented out a cheap room in Boulaq Aboulela and brought his wife Sultana up from the country to live with him on whatever they could earn. After seven years they had their only child, Ahmed—seven years in which Shaker had aged and grown thin. Sultana, though, remained plump: beneath an outer layer of poverty and neglect, her powerful, well-knit frame grew ever sturdier, prompting her Cairene neighbours to claim she must eat her husband's portion.

Shaker would meet my grandfather often, the pair of them sitting on the pavement outside the Valley of the Kings Café which looked out over Abdeen Square; my grandfather in his dapper grey suit and Shaker in the simple *galabeyya* that emphasized his gaunt frame. They'd sit through the afternoon and past supper, till night calmly came down over the still oasis that was Cairo of the thirties, caught up in a long conversation in which they'd switch between Arabic and Nubian with an impalpable fluidity, responding to the confidentiality of the subject under discussion or the degree of verbal abstraction it required. Nubian was for quotidian concerns and family matters, for intimacy and a precautionary impenetrability when discussing such things amid strangers. Arabic was for public affairs and topics of a more rarified bent (Nubian's primitive and artless nature meant it was almost totally devoid of conceptual terms) which by and large meant religion, a subject both of them, each in his own way, were deeply interested in, even though Shaker, while unflaggingly observant, had never set foot in a mosque or prayed in company, which he justified on the grounds that we all go to our Lord alone.

When those of our female relatives who had also settled in Cairo paid visits to my grandmother, they would sniff at the relationship between my grandfather (the effendi, the educated, the gainfully employed) and the idiot Shaker whose foolhardiness had been a byword back in the day, back in what came to be known as 'the old country'.

The contrast between the two characters seemed obvious and was unsettling even within the confines of the Nubian ghetto, which looked tolerantly on friendships based on ethnic and tribal ties that might cross lines of class and education. My grandmother would mutter in Nubian, defending her husband, saying that blood can never turn to water and mentioning the Prophet's advice to look to one's family first. But the older and wiser women spoke of a near drowning that had almost carried my grandfather away as a young boy and of Shaker saving him from certain death, the time the two of them had held a swimming race across the Nile back in the old country, in the old days. My grandfather defended Shaker on the grounds that he was enlightened: despite his extreme poverty and want of education, he not only bought and read books but also evinced a talent for memorizing the genealogical tree to which his family belonged—births and deaths and every individual twig: who had remained in the old country and who had emigrated south to Sudan and north to Cairo after the construction of the Aswan Dam.

Before long, my grandfather's hopes for his friend ran into obstacles. Shaker's fortunes went into decline and the doubts about him started to seem justified. He had joined a Sufi order which he claimed was combatting black magic and which was in all likelihood one of those secret groups that infested interwar Cairo, conducting their esoteric activities under cover of Sufism.

Prompted by curiosity, my grandfather's nephew Fathi went with Shaker to attend one of the order's gatherings and, on his return, said that it had been unlike any other Sufi gathering he'd ever been to, north or south. Those present had not sat on the ground as brothers of an order are wont to do, but altogether, at a round table, respectable gentleman alongside men of exceptionally modest means such as Shaker, and at their head a fearsome sheikh, who no sooner caught sight of Fathi than he insisted that he leave their circle, since no imbiber of alcohol might sit among them. Fathi swore that he hadn't sampled any for three nights prior—which by sheer chance was the truth—and he was unable to say what keen-eyed observation or intuition had led the sheikh to tear the veil from his private life.

Aside from that one brief insight into Shaker's tireless activities with the order, his world and his movements within it remained a secret impenetrable even to those closest to him, including my grandfather who frequently pressed him to reveal something of what he did. To which Shaker's unvarying response was that he, in particular, must keep his distance from that world.

Shaker gave himself over entirely to the order and, bit by bit, began to neglect his domestic duties. He took extended absences from work. He became thinner, too, his features growing darker and more indistinct, and he would walk the streets in tatters, so that anyone who saw him flitting between the shadows of the city centre's towering buildings or the gloom of Boulaq's damp alleys might think him a phantom. He lost his job due to his continual absences and the crisis came to touch on the most basic needs of his household. It became clear that Shaker would never be fit to reenter steady employment now that his spiritual inclinations had come to consume his entire being and he was unable to attend to the most quotidian duties, so Sultana went knocking on neighbours' doors begging for help. It was at this juncture that my grandfather intervened in Shaker's life for the final time, forcing him to quit Cairo and return to the south: to gather up his things and take with him Sultana, young Ahmed and a metal trunk packed with yellowed books.

The government had compensated the residents of the village from which my grandfather came (and which was now entombed beneath the waters of the Aswan Dam) with land around the hamlet of Al Toud in the Luxor municipality, to the south of that city, halfway to Esna. On one part of his lot, my grandfather had built a house beside a hill from which one could survey the sugarcane plantations stretching away and the Nile which lay about a kilometre distant—quite unlike the old country, where their houses had overlooked the water. On the western horizon, beyond the river, the peaks around Gurna soared. Aside from the occasional holiday, when my grandfather would take some or all of the family to spend a few days down in Al Toud, the house sat empty, as did many of the village's other houses whose owners, like my grandfather, had emigrated north with a minority heading south to Wadi Halfa, which would be submerged in turn some years later.

So Shaker and his family repaired to the house with orders from my grandfather to do what he could with his modest plot, in addition to whatever he could manage of my grandfather's share, and to live on the proceeds. This, so my grandfather imagined, would bring an end to the sorry tale, but the curse that had afflicted Shaker in Cairo rode with him those many miles south and within days it was possible to observe the quantitative and qualitative difference between his crops and those tended by his neighbours—Nubians and Southerners who, if anything, farmed even less land than Shaker's few acres.

He was never a farmer: Sultana's excuse, offered to neighbours and relatives who came to commiserate and gloat. Shaker's excuse was that he had set himself on a path of no return; that he was set on his way even if it meant destruction. Thus the content of the concise, clipped letter he sent in response to my grandfather's missive of blame and censure.

It was claimed at the time that Shaker had entered into occult battle with a sorcerer from Assiut. This was deemed sufficient explanation for his lack of children and the poverty of his crop. It ended with him confined to the inner rooms of the house in Al Toud where the winds of hunger might garner nothing from the smooth tiles of his thin body, hiding for days with his trunk of books and a frightened Sultana listening to the sound of soft whimpering and weeping while young Ahmed cowered in her lap.

At last, one summer's midnight, there was the sound of a tremendous commotion and he emerged. Sultana came running with her gas lantern to find him standing in the living room knocking a nail into the wall with a lump of rock and moaning as though wrestling with some great internal pain. She approached him, lantern held high, and warily, sadly, whispered his name twice. The instant she touched his back, he screamed, rocketing upright and, knocking the lantern from her hand, sprinted out of the front door.

Shaker left the house that midnight, traversed the little hill and hid himself from Sultana's sight in the heart of the desert. Swallowed up. He was never seen again. And standing beside the house, young Ahmed—clinging to the tail of his mother's black robe.

The news deeply saddened my grandfather and he took to his room. After the legally prescribed number of months had passed, Sultana was able to obtain a court ruling that Shaker was 'absent' and she was thereby divorced from him, and, after another three months, she married Bakheit, also a relative of hers, in keeping with custom. And Bakheit, with his cheerful personality and shrewd strategies for weathering life's storms, managed to make her forget the years of fear and anxiety she'd spent with Shaker.

My grandfather, feeling himself morally obliged to adopt the young boy, summoned Ahmed from Al Toud to Cairo but not before promising Sultana—and prior to that, himself—that he would take responsibility for raising and educating the child until he could find a path for himself through life. Young Ahmed would live with his children, like one of them, his rights and duties (so full of good intentions!) no different from theirs.

But Ahmed Shaker was about five years younger than the youngest of my grandfather's sons and this fact conspired with the orphan complex that afflicted him (despite himself, and despite the best intentions of others) to place him in a position somewhere between baby and servant in the domestic hierarchy. When he was still a boy the other sons were teenagers, and when he became a teen they were young men. Who was going to help the woman (my grandmother) with the housework, now that she was getting old, and who was going to buy the bread and vegetables from the Ithnein Market near Nasiriya—other than young Ahmed? And when my grandfather sought to give him a start, to turn him over to the study of religion and the Koran, he put him into the Azharite education system, thereby setting him at two removes from his real children, all of whom had been enrolled in the state system from the outset. It has always been the case that an Azharite education is less expensive.

It was here, without anyone quite intending it, that the seed was sown of Ahmed Shaker's breach with the family beneath whose wing he'd sheltered. In the rift that opened up his self-consciousness and his otherness gathered force and, upon reaching the first year of middle school (Azharite, too, off course), Ahmed went off of his own accord and took work as an apprentice to a tailor on whose door he'd seen an advertisement for a keen-eyed boy to help out in the shop. Ahmed knew himself to possess excellent vision compared to my grandfather's children (that is, my father and uncles) who had inherited their poor eyesight from their father. He would spend the morning picking his way through Shaafite jurisprudence and the Alfiyya of Ibn Malik and the afternoon hand-stitching articles his master would finish off with his Singer sewing machine. No sooner had Ahmed completed his high-school certificate and enrolled at Al Azhar University (Department of Commerce) than he left my grandfather's house altogether, and, registered as a boarding student from Aswan, put up in a small room in the Tekkiya of Mohamed Bey Aboul Dahab, which used to function as a boarding house for the university before the Antiquities Department had it registered as a national monument. By now he had qualified as a *maqassdar*, a guild rank that enabled him to take work with a moderately well-off tailor in Bateniya who could guarantee him a respectable income, particularly over the holiday season and at the start of the school year.

In a parallel history, my father and his siblings had married and I had been born. By the time of Ahmed Shaker's final appearance, I was a bouncing infant. This appearance took place at the wake held for my grandfather in the mid-seventies, after which Ahmed Shaker never again showed his face at any family gathering. The last we heard—my youngest uncle had bumped into him on Qasr El Ainy Street—he'd finally graduated after ten years divided between the tailor's in Bateniya and his residence at Mohamed Aboul Dahab, which he'd been forced to leave when the Antiquities Department requisitioned it, going to live in a room in Derasa, then getting a job as a third-rank accountant at the Department for Social Security while continuing his work as a tailor in the evenings to make ends meet.

Midway through my time at university, I had fixed on the idea of myself as a writer and spent most of my days drifting about carrying a brown leather satchel containing paper, pens and a few novels and books of poetry, and making a tour of the coffee shops. Café Rex in Emad El Din Street was a daily port of call. I'd sit in the outside enclosure located—before it and the whole cafe were consigned to oblivion—on a side street linking Emad El Din Street with Zakariya Ahmed (formerly Galal Street). The patrons who frequented this enclosure were most of them eccentrics, and they lent the place a timeless atmosphere. I'd sit by myself for hours, smoking like a writer and, like a writer, scrutinizing the faces of my fellow patrons. I would read passages from the books I had brought and attempt to write lines of verse, sometimes successfully and sometimes not.

I didn't immediately recognize his face. He was sitting at a table at one end of the enclosure, next to the food stall that belonged to the cafe, and eating a bowl of macaroni to which had been added black cubes of liver fried in oil. He ate without enthusiasm, as though refuelling for the journey ahead. Line by line, his features returned to my memory, rising from a bottomless abyss and surfacing, to fit over the face of the man chewing his food just a few metres away. The same slender, black face.

As he finished the final spoonful, he became aware of my gaze. He looked disconcerted, then, rapidly paying the waiter for his food, he left. I remembered that he worked at the Social Security Department which lay nearby, and I was sure it was him, but it never occurred to me that he might have recognized me. He hadn't seen me since I was a baby.

More than a minute passed between his leaving and the moment I decided to go after him. Less than a minute for me to pay the bill for my coffee, gather my papers into the leather satchel and set off in pursuit. But by the time I turned into Alfi Street, where I'd guessed he'd gone, he had already reached Orabi Square, heading for Tawfiqiya. I saw his back moving away into the crowds, striding fast, almost at a trot, and glancing over his shoulder like a fugitive. I was trying to catch him up, that face with its blurred features which brought back to me the memory of an old, old tale, while he . . . he was fleeing, too: from old, familiar features; the faces of my father and uncles that haunted my own.